A SMALL PROBLEM

Written by Cas Lester

THE BAD GUYS

Enoch

Howell

Enoch's men

3

Ben and Gwen were at the Riptide Rapid Zone – a massive water park with the biggest splash-slide ever! MEGA COOL!
"What a shame," said Gwen smugly. "You're too small to go on this ride!"

Ben was angry. When no one was watching, he used the Omnitrix to turn into Grey Matter. He sneaked onto the splash-slide next to Gwen, and they whizzed down to the pool.

"Grandpa will be *so* mad at you," said Gwen. "I'll just turn back," said Grey Matter, "so he won't even know!"

But before Grey Matter could turn back into Ben, a stranger grabbed him.

"Hey!" yelled Gwen. "Let him go!" Gwen told Grandpa what had happened, and they raced after the man.

The man jumped into his
car and drove off.

"Oh no!" cried Gwen.

"Don't worry," said Grandpa,
"we'll find Grey Matter."

On the other side of town, the man, Howell, had taken Grey Matter back home. "Wow! A real alien," Howell said excitedly. "You are going to make me rich!"

"Dream on!" said Grey Matter.

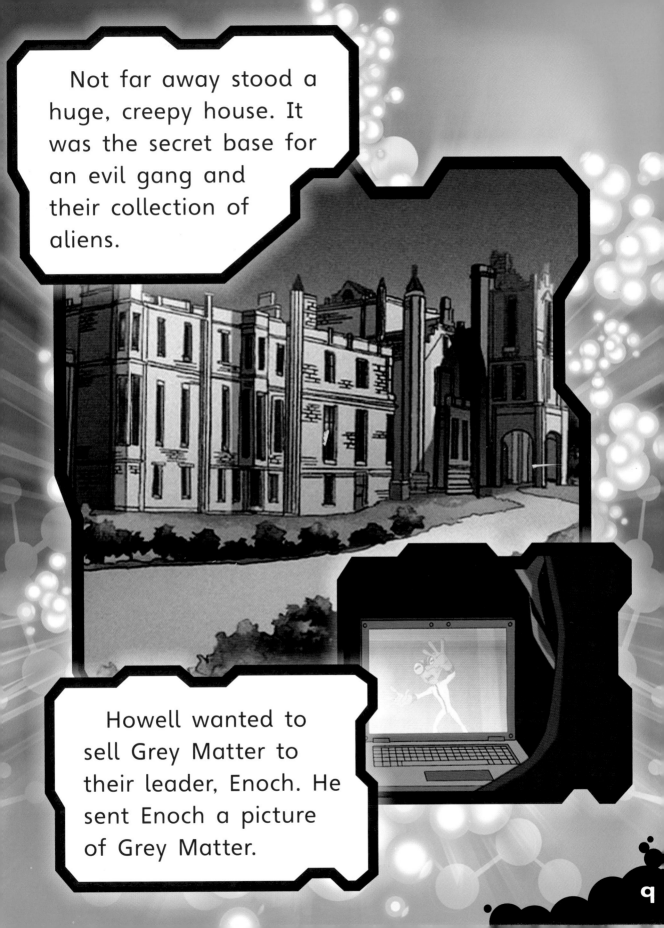

Not far away stood a huge, creepy house. It was the secret base for an evil gang and their collection of aliens.

Howell wanted to sell Grey Matter to their leader, Enoch. He sent Enoch a picture of Grey Matter.

But Grey Matter had other ideas! He got the cat to knock the jar onto the floor. It smashed and Grey Matter escaped.

Gwen and Grandpa were driving round the town looking for Howell's car.

"If we can find it," said Grandpa, "we can find Grey Matter."

Back at Howell's house, Grey Matter could see the name of the street where he was trapped. He found a phone and quickly called Gwen.

But suddenly ...

Grey Matter was trapped again! "This is *so* not going to plan!" he groaned.

Gwen found the street on the map. "We're nearly there!" she said. "Hurry!"

But Enoch's men had already arrived at Howell's house to buy Grey Matter.

Enoch's men put Grey Matter in a glass box and got back into their car. They raced off in a cloud of smoke.

The car pulled up at the secret base. When Enoch saw Grey Matter, he was pleased. "What an interesting alien!" he said. "I will keep it forever."

Grandpa and Gwen arrived at Howell's house, but it was too late. Gwen saw something lying on the ground. "It's Howell's phone!" she said. "If we can trace this number, we can track down Enoch and his men."

They traced the number to the secret base. Gwen stared at the creepy old house.

"This is not good news for Grey Matter," said Grandpa. He knew all about Enoch and his evil ways.

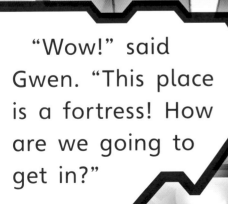

"Wow!" said Gwen. "This place is a fortress! How are we going to get in?"

"This is not your best idea, Grandpa!" said Gwen.

"Got a better one?" asked Grandpa.

CLANG!

A guard met them at the top of the wall. Grandpa quickly got rid of him. Then he and Gwen rushed inside to look for Grey Matter.

Inside the house, Grey Matter had escaped from the glass box. Now he was trying to get away from Enoch's men.

Then Grey Matter bumped into Gwen's leg.

"Grey Matter! You're safe!" said Gwen.

But Grandpa had heard Enoch's men coming. "Quick, in here!" he said, and they slipped through a door.

Some lights snapped on and they found themselves in a room full of alien weapons.

"We must destroy everything," said Grey Matter.

Then ... BLAST! Enoch and his men burst through the door. "Catch them!" shouted Enoch.

Grey Matter told Gwen and Grandpa to get out. Then he climbed deep inside one of the weapons. He fixed the wires so that the weapon would explode in ten seconds ...

Enoch saw what Grey Matter was doing. "Everybody get out!" he ordered. "This place is about to blow up!"

FTZZZ!

KABOOM!

Suddenly, the Omnitrix turned Grey Matter back into Ben and he raced outside, just in time.

"It was cool being a little alien. I really made things go with a bang at Enoch's house!" said Ben. "But it's even more cool to be big again!"

"Big? Huh!" laughed Gwen. "You're still just a shrimp!"